Praise for *Honk*

Jim has created a thought-provoking and powerful allegory that prompts us to reflect deeply on our own mission and our own leadership journey. I couldn't help thinking about my family, my team, and my business as I followed the journey shared in *Honk*.

In short form, Jim reminds us all just how connected we are to the universe around us and how nature often provides the finest example of a pure, highly functioning team.

Verne Harnish
Founder, Entrepreneurs' Organization (EO)
and author of *Start to Scale*

Honk is beautifully written: like the perfect fall day, it is both clear and crisp. This leadership journey provides inspiration, insights, and clarity on what is important. The wisdom Jim shares sets the conditions for every reader to gain valuable lessons in leadership and life, regardless of whether they are leading themselves or others. A timeless story, both entertaining and thought-provoking!

Dean A. DiSibio
Colonel, U.S. Army (Retired)
Founder of Colonels Leadership Council and co-author of
Reel Lessons in Leadership

Honk is an incredible story for all ages that blends a journey of self-discovery and awareness with the truths and challenges of leadership. These truths are applicable to veteran leaders as well as those just learning to navigate new leadership roles. Jim adds just the right touch of storytelling and mystery in the adventure. Loved it!

Tom Saunders, Ph.D.
Author of *Choices, Decisions that Last a Lifetime* and of
The Road between Us, the Elder and the Atheist
Veteran leadership trainer and management consultant
for over 35 years

Honk is a wonderful story filled with a richness we don't see often. You can't wait for the next chapter. I found myself emotionally attached to the characters and immediately invested. The journey carries messaging that sticks for some time.

Susan Waring Koch
Senior Banking Executive and co-author of
If It Comes in a Black Velvet Box, I'll Love It!

HONK

sound
wisdom.
Because Your Success Matters

HONK

A LEADERSHIP JOURNEY OF LOVE, HOPE, AND JOY

JAMES E. DECARLO

Published and distributed by:

SOUND WISDOM
P.O. Box 310
Shippensburg, PA 17257-0310

717-530-2122

info@soundwisdom.com

www.soundwisdom.com

Jacket design by Joe Brooks at JWB & Co.

ISBN 13 TP: 978-1-64095-636-0

ISBN 13 eBook: 978-1-64095-637-7

For Worldwide Distribution, Printed in the U.S.A.

1 2 3 4 5 6 7 8 / 29 28 27 26 25

*To Art and Mary, for encouraging
me to write—and for being the
finest benchmark of Love, Hope,
and Joy I've ever witnessed.*

Mom and Dad, may you rest in peace.

"Freedom is when the work we do is no longer work, and our efforts form part of a bigger system at play—a system that we feel connected to."

—Old Radar

Contents

CHAPTER 1

Great leaders don't
dwell on the past,
they move forward.

Haunted

He was told that a good decision is anchored in *reason*. Leaders are charged with making decisions all the time, sometimes without all the information, relying on gut instinct.

He was also told that all leaders make mistakes, that they learn from these moments. Great leaders don't dwell on the past, they move forward.

He can hear the wisdom of these words circling in his head, whirling around and around—screaming at him. "So why can't I let this go!" he shouts out loud to no one. He coughs from his own folly. Feeling totally alone, he is gripped by the torment of his own leadership. Droplets of blood spill into the water from the corner of his beak.

Looking down, wiping the blood away, he thinks to himself, *Get it together, Hummer! In a few hours you will have an entire flock to lead south.* Another cough. He whispers into the dark air, "I'll be fine," as if willing himself to be well.

Her small, private cove is dark and hidden. She likes it like that. On the cove's embankment she keeps their photo protected from the elements. It's all she has left of her parents.

She can often hear other members of the flock playing, talking, and moving about just over the other side of her private area. They leave her alone for the most part. They respect her request for privacy...even today, almost a year later.

I've never taken a trip like this without you, she says to herself, looking at the picture as if hoping for a response. Looking to the heavens she utters into the darkness, "Who will be here for you if I leave?"

The young goose circles in her small cove, reflecting and praying, as she has done for months. She pauses, looking over at the photo of her parents, flattened by her own thoughts: *Who am I kidding. You are never coming back, and no one hears me.*

CHAPTER 2

Sometimes we must
do things we don't
want to do.... And it only
works when we all show
up, young and old.

A Journey Begins

W e move out tomorrow!" blared Hummer, a member of the Leadership Council in charge of the annual migration. "The time has come for us *all* to migrate to our warmer climate in Tampa, Florida. Wheels up tomorrow at 0500," emphasizing the word *all*. In eleven hours, this flock of geese would be 9,500 feet above sea level, flying in a perfect V-formation and honking back and forth with one another for almost four days.

"Why do I have to go?" Jet asked Hummer, cornering him as he stepped away after addressing the gaggle.

"Because you are a part of this flock! It's that simple, Jet." He turned to leave, stopping mid-stride and swinging back to look her straight in the eye, "Sometimes we must do things we don't want to do, that's just part of life, and part of growing up. You play a role in this migration south. We all do! And it only works when we all show up, young and old."

Feeling invalidated, Jet coldly responded, "Not everyone is a fan of heading south so early in the Fall, Hummer! Many in this flock are used to a little chill in the air and the Leadership Council never chose *September* for the annual migration. From what I understand, October, and even November, are better migration months, less risk of storms off the Atlantic."

Hummer didn't budge, "Soon this area will see frost regularly, and some parts fully frozen. The cold you feel now won't let up! Damn it, Jet, the cold just continues to get worse when winter sets in properly." Then, with almost a touch of exhaustion in his voice, he added, "And, these days, winter hits us in a flash. The food supply for a flock our size is depleted from the first frost...and that frost has already hit, Jet."

Jet took a breath to say something, but Hummer cut her off, a note of irritation in his voice, "We can't afford to take another chance this year."

On that, she just stared at Hummer. Hummer, himself, was stung by his own words falling from his mouth. Jet had no response. In that moment, with the two of them alone, standing there after the assembly, you could cut the air with a knife. Neither had any words to offer. Emotions were high. With that, feeling he had said too much, he pivoted and abruptly left the discussion—shutting down any reply, coldly leaving Jet standing alone.

But Jet was unable to see the pain on Hummer's face as he headed away. Likewise, Hummer was unaware that Jet, weakened by the intense emotions overwhelming her, had let go of her immense inner strength. Tears rolled down her cheeks. An agonizing pain welled up from a sudden wave of sadness, disabling her, as her throat closed with a burning sensation. She could hardly breathe from the grief inside. Her powerful body convulsing in a silent sob, "I miss you so much," she whispered as if someone were listening.

Hummer's declaration, *we can't afford to take another chance this year,* reverberated in her ears and unpacked a flood of emotion that she had held back since the time when her parents joined a small expedition to the most eastern shores of Maine. The group of four, assigned to be a reconnaissance team for the flock, was tasked with finding an Autumn location, safe enough and warm enough between Bar Harbor and Portland, Maine. The right coastal area would give the flock more time in the northeast before a winter freeze, granting them a few more weeks and allowing the annual hurricane season to pass.

They knew of other flocks of geese that took to these coastal waters—reporting only good things about the warmer coastline water, the bountiful food sources, and a topography offering gentle beauty.

Jet's parents were expert explorers and rushed to sign up for the short expedition southeast of their home in Quebec. The whole trip was meant to take the four geese seven days: two there, two back, and three days between the two boundary points. A snap-frost hit hard while they were away; a cold front from the mid-Atlantic to Nova Scotia lasted almost five days. The temperatures were in the 30s. These temperatures recorded the coldest five days for September ever, and no one saw it coming. Exhausted, with a limited food supply, all four volunteers never returned home.

Jet remembered just resting quietly for days after it became clear her parents were not coming home—blaming the Leadership Council for allowing the expedition to happen. Nobody offered an explanation or even an apology, just condolences. She remembered the darkness in her soul and feeling so alone. And now, Hummer suddenly dropped a comment like that: "we can't afford to take another chance this year." *Did he kill my parents by sending them to Maine? Did the Leadership Council know the dangers? Why?*

Later that night Jet arranged her belongings to prepare for the journey ahead. She had no idea what to expect. Drawn by emotion, she wrote a few words:

> I hate this! And I hate them! Why do I need to go to Tampa? I DON'T NEED ANYONE ELSE! I prefer being alone. Why can't they see that?

She tried to sleep, knowing that within hours the city of Quebec would be behind them, including the icy mornings bringing in the sudden winter chill and shrouded with memories that still haunt her. Jet knew she had to go, but she didn't like it.

At 5:00 the next morning, with the gaggle standing on the point at Sainte-Petronille, Hummer again addressed the group. "We are strong when we operate as one. Under normal conditions, I would expect that this flock could travel 1,500 miles in 24 hours. But these are not normal conditions, we have the entire community with us on this migration, some young and, well, some not so young. Given that we are departing today, we are in no rush. The plan is to take it slow and fly as one flock. The good news is that we will not need to long-haul it to Florida."

The news of a slower pace was exciting for many, with some in the group of 33 loudly applauding Hummer.

"We will fly as one flock with a few stops along the old southern route. As such, the Leadership Council has put each of you, including me, in small teams. If anyone needs help, food, feels unwell, or just needs to stop for any reason, that team will go to ground as a unit while the rest of us will fly on more slowly, allowing them a chance to catch up.

"One more thing! This year I will start at the back of the flock and then gradually work my way toward the front to support the drafting program. Just honk if you need me."

The group found Hummer's last statement unsettling—Hummer typically led the annual migration for the flock. Predicting this reaction he quickly added, "I've asked other senior members from the leadership team to lead us off. As you know, with years under their well-worn belt, our elders are more experienced travelers with a firm grasp on the route from Quebec to Tampa, Florida. We are in good hands!" Reading the flock and noticing a sense of sudden ease, he added, "I want to thank you all for your leadership and co-operation as we embark on this journey!" Looking over in Jet's direction as he finished, "It takes each and every one of us, working together, to migrate this distance. Let's roll!"

Moments later members of the group began honking. Slowly, others joined in. The gaggle built both pitch and momentum with the sound of piercing honks bouncing off the water. The honking reached a crescendo just as Hummer took to the air and others followed. Chaos at first! The birds circled to find both space and team members. To Jet, the scene was a total circus, and she laughed out loud at the entropy surrounding her before joining the group above. The flock suddenly seemed to spread out, almost naturally and without command. Hummer slid directly behind Jet in the V formation; she immediately realized she was teaming up with *him* for the migration south.

As the St. Lawrence River below them fell away, she thought about their last exchange. Still unsure how she felt about it all, they did not talk, suiting her mood.

CHAPTER 3

All teams need good leadership to set the goals and strategy that a group believes in. Once a team has firm confidence in the purpose and in the direction they are heading, then we all, in our own way, become leaders.

High Wisdom

Above 10,000 feet, almost four hours since take off, the flock of 33 was high above Sherbrook, 100 miles due south from Quebec City when the honking began again. The flock honked incessantly before reshuffling the V-formation, resetting the flying sequence, and relieving the leading elder since the start at Sainte-Petronille.

Settling into this new order throughout a V-shape formation, Jet noticed Hummer's choice to remain in place at the rear of the flock. Then, they were joined by a much older, very powerful looking gander. He introduced himself as Radar and slipped in behind Hummer. Sensing an energy of friction between Hummer and Jet passing down to him, Radar was happy to silently glide in the draft of the long V-formation.

A short time passed, and finally, while looking east toward the haunting Maine shoreline, trying not to think about her parents, Jet asked the most basic question—a stark reminder that this was her maiden migration. Breaking silence, she asked, "Why do we fly like this?"

"The V-formation is the most optimal for any team of geese," Radar offered up, in a naturally gravelly but smooth voice. "When flying long distances over a mix of mountains, plains, and water, you need all eyes on whatever is ahead.

This formation gives us that. We are spread wide with each team member having equal visibility."

Hummer took a moment to respond and answered, "Great teams work together by collaborating on what they see. This helps them to achieve their overarching goal and navigate obstacles that present themselves along the way. No one member of the team or any one group should have more or less visibility than another. That leads to poor performance caused by a lack of information which in turn increases risk for everyone." Hummer looked at Jet happy to reengage with her. She remained cold.

"Equal visibility? What's that all about?" she murmured.

Radar jumped in, "Jet, I bet you thought it was for drafting purposes only?" She couldn't believe he just said that—it was *exactly* what she was thinking. "Humans calculate that flying in a V-formation provides us with a 71 percent increased flying range produced by the updraft from those around us. I don't know about any of that," Radar continued, "we've simply learned over the eons that when you share a common vision, a clear direction, and operate with a sense of community, we all get to our destination quicker and more efficiently."

Speaking with more curiosity, she asked, "Why all the honking then if everyone knows where we are going?"

"Encouragement and community," said Hummer. "Being near the front of the V-formation is hard work. The front sets the pace for the rest of us. We honk to encourage those in front to keep up their effort. And when one team member falls out of formation it creates an immediate drag slowing down the entire group. The sound of our encouraging honks helps the entire flock stay together."

Jet flew on in silence, as if still ignoring Hummer, but she could not ignore his heavy breathing. *He's half the age of Old Radar!* she thought. Looking back to Radar, drafting at the back of the flock, his long wingspan moving in rhythm to hers, she smiled at the old gander and privately thought, *I think Old Radar is a more suitable name.*

Radar recognized in the moment that some of the more subtle but important lessons of flying as a group might be missed on Jet. So, after a few moments he added, "Jet, all teams need good leadership to set the goals and strategy that a group believes in. Once a team has firm confidence in the purpose and in the direction they are heading, then we all, in our own way, become leaders. Hummer touched on this when he thanked everyone in assembly before the flock took off today. I think it was '*No role is more important or less important than another.*'" He paused again, intentionally going slowly for Jet to take it all in.

"Jet, a true leader is not always at the front of the V, but sometimes in the middle with the rest of us providing guidance, encouragement, insight, and helping to foster innovative solutions and increased collaboration. Then again, sometimes leadership shows up whenever a team member steps in to help another, either when asked or not asked. Good leadership has many forms."

"Like taking the front of the V-formation when it's needed, helping to share the load and cut through the headwind," Jet said, more as a question in her voice.

"Exactly! Leadership is not by title or rank—that's power, and power is always short-lived. Good leaders serve others to allow them to do their job, and in a way, this serves the broader team goal." Looking down at the streets below him, he added, "Humans often engage with displays of power. In fact, they seem to relish power struggles. This thirst for dominance is driven by ego, pride, and constructs of greed that don't exist among our type in the animal kingdom. As geese, we work together in good times and in difficult times—as one! Envy, keeping score, and material need is not an evil in our veins."

Jet looked down to see a high school gridiron game taking place below them. She chuckled at the coach yelling at the referee. Parents screaming as well. Radar looked over to her and said sarcastically, "My point, exactly."

As all 33 continued heading southeast Radar and Jet could not ignore Hummer had yet to offer to move their team forward in the flock. It was clear he was struggling during this first day.

"Jet, there is another reason we use the V-formation when we fly as a team," Hummer said as they crossed over New

Hampshire in the direction of Boston, leveraging some common ground to keep the conversation going. "As I mentioned to the flock before we left Quebec, when a goose gets sick or is wounded, others can drop from the team V-formation to protect and support that bird until it is able to fly again. They then use a smaller V to launch again, either directly catching up with the flock or by joining another group to draft with."

"That's important, Jet, each member of each team needs the other," Radar added, making eye contact with Jet—who suddenly felt the old gander almost looking into her soul.

"I had no idea the V-formation for a flock of geese had so much behind it." Jet's words were barely heard. As she spoke, the honking in the group was growing louder and louder. Boston metro was now in sight, the final travel destination for the first day was close. The flock had found calm waters to rest in for the night. Spot Pond was a wide body of water in a preserve just north of Boston, and near the famous Stone Zoo and teeming with wildlife. On cue, as in the takeoff 14 hours earlier, the flock fell out of formation, and the landing descended into chaos. Jet joined the circus and descended as best she could onto the water. A few minutes later, after all the geese were accounted for, Hummer gently landed next to her.

Catching his breath, he turned and spoke softly. "I'm sorry, Jet. I want to apologize for my words yesterday. I didn't intend to hurt you." Jet found it impossible to remain cold toward Hummer, given all she learned about her species, about teams earlier in the day, and especially from Old Radar's scorching comment that we all need each other. She turned slowly to truly look at Hummer for the first time since they took off.

"I can't imagine what you went through last year. And I can't imagine what you might *still* be dealing with from your parents not returning home," he said. Tears filled her eyes, but he continued speaking. He was forced to pause to compose himself, and to give her space as the tears fell. "The Leadership Council may have approved the expedition, but I ratified it. And when they didn't return...well, that decision to let them go has been haunting me ever since. I feel personally responsible and trapped by that fact and that I can't change any of it." He caught his breath. "I'm so sorry, Jet...and when you said you didn't want to join us, and tried to argue that we should wait a few more weeks, it was all too much. The risk of staying and being hit again by a fluke cold spell, like the very one that hit Maine last year during the expedition... Well, I exploded, and I shouldn't have. Jet, I'm sorry. I hope you can forgive me." His voice trailed off as he worked hard to hold back his own feelings.

A darkness in the pit of her heart, the darkness she had been suppressing for almost twelve months, kept her from forming a reply. She tried. But in the end, feeling confused, she gently swam away wondering if he just asked forgiveness for losing her parents. Yet, somewhere deep inside she was pleased to hear the most genuine, generous, and honest apology she never thought would come.

As the night fell, she pulled out her journal to capture her heavy feelings and what mattered most from the day:

I'm not sure why I'm stuck with Hummer, but I'll take it. He apologized. It felt right.

I learned something today that will last a lifetime:

> A good team has good leadership, and everyone has a role to play.

> Only with a clear goal shared by all does a team work best together.

> Good leaders don't try to control others.

> Geese honk with purpose! We need each other along the way.

CHAPTER 4

We learn from mistakes,
and it's encouraged...
each trusting the other,
the workplace thrives
in perfect harmony.

Small Lessons

Early the next morning as Jet woke on the water, she immediately noticed Old Radar with a small branch in his beak. He was on the edge of the shore hustling downstream carrying the branch, a couple of leaves hanging off it. He was staring down at three large ants, floating below him. He ran to outpace the current and tossed the twig into the water. Jet watched as the three ants climbed up onto the branch and the water coasted it onto shore. There, on dry land, the ants hopped off and went on their way.[1]

Catching up to him, she asked, "What was *that* all about?" Jet's tone displayed her naïveté.

He looked at her, wondering if she was asking *why* he was being kind to strangers or why he was being kind to the *ants*. "Jet, Mother Nature operates through an ecosystem that is all connected. The ants, just like trees, and that fungus growing on those rocks over there, play an important role in our broader universe. We are no more important than them, or the superorganisms around us, and vice versa. They are no more important than us. We all work together to form a balance. Ants matter." He then paused. He could tell she wasn't buying it, doubting him.

---

1. Sara Gruen, *Water for Elephants* (Algonquin Books, 2006).

"Earlier, before you awoke, I was observing that ant colony just beyond those trees. Like us, this larger colony operates in small teams. Each group's distinctive work contributes to the success of the wider colony. Ant colonies can have almost 200,000 ants in them, each member carrying a different role while working in their set team." His smooth voice seemed almost inspired. "Did you know that for over 100 million years ants have been continuing to adapt and survive through their complex and evolving social structures? They are fascinating to observe, but you must know what to look for."

"Radar, they are just ants, c'mon—what can we learn from an ant colony?"

He ignored her innocent comment. "Anyway, those three guys were blown into the water while I was watching them scout for food. And I felt a duty to help," he paused to make sure what he was about to say was abundantly clear, "...and I helped because I could. It was the right thing to do."

Just then the winds changed abruptly, and the sky darkened. The tall pines surrounding the lake leaned from the force. It triggered Radar's instincts as he immediately knew these conditions could be dangerous. He swung around to look southeast and saw a large storm brewing fast and heading their way. *Not good*, thought Radar. They would need to move and move quickly if they were going to get around this weather system. He had no idea what they faced, but he could tell it carried a punch.

Radar and Jet discovered Hummer still in his tucked sleep position as they approached him to share the news of bad weather in the area. Radar circled in the water as Hummer slowly lifted his head, his eyes unwell. Hummer looked at Jet and pushed out, "I'm not able to fly today. I'm sorry, I'm just not feeling well enough."

Radar moved closer to Jet and cautiously whispered, "Jet, this is not an option. No can do. We've got to move! That storm off the Atlantic coast is brewing and suddenly moving our way. We need to be in the air in the next few minutes if we are going to get around this thing," there was urgency in his voice. Jet nudged Hummer and repeated the message.

"I can't. I understand if you want to take off with the rest of the flock. I'll be fine. I just need a day to rest." He laid his head back under his wing, protected in the cove and unaware of the imminent storm.

By now, the entire gaggle had been a witness to the storm winds and gray skies. The Leadership Council met briefly in the cove to discuss a strategy. They laid out two options; leave Hummer behind for a day and move the rest of the flock southwest using a new, more inland, direction; or stay together on the lake and risk the young and old with the storm. Some debate occurred.

"There's another option," Jet interjected. "He's my team! And I say we stay back together to let him regain his strength while the rest of you get a jump against the squall, taking the safer inland route."

The Leadership Council went silent. Jet added, "Don't let my maiden migration be a factor here. We are a team!" She shot a look at Old Radar to feed off his confidence. "I got this," she said. "Go!"

Moments later, with the Leadership Council honking directions for all, the flock took to the air. This time, Jet witnessed 30 geese in more order than she recalled from the first time they took off as a group. She wondered if it was like this the first time but she just hadn't noticed. Meanwhile the increasing cloud covering combined with high wind speeds became a threat to everyone's safety. The storm was moving in fast. After five minutes or so, the flock was away and almost out of sight, heading more west than south—intentionally inland and away from the storm. Jet felt a warm relief knowing they were safe.

When Hummer lifted his head to see Jet at his side, he gave out a gentle honk, and together they moved under shelter deeper in the cove, back in the direction of the ants, safe from the storm.

"So now what?" asked Jet. "What the heck! Are the three of us now going to fly directly into a storm?" A worrying tone in her voice, as she addressed Old Radar.

"Not happening, young lady. Chill out, rookie! We're going to see this storm out right here with Hummer and,

God willing, he's ready to fly tomorrow," adding, "besides, all major storms or hurricanes pass overhead in less than 24 hours, so we should be good to go."

Time passed while the winds continued increasing around them as the storm approached. Radar was certain the flock's new route southwest would work well, given his calculations on the size and direction of the storm. More inland than usual, but confident a southwest route will work.

Hummer rested.

"Hey, were you being serious about the ants and the whole thing about the universe being connected?" Jet shot Radar with a look of "*Really?*" on her face along with a quizzical look indicating an intent to learn more.

"Come with me." They left Hummer sleeping while he helped Jet up the side of the water's edge, bringing her around to the area where he stood earlier in the day, locating the ant colony. "Let's just pause here for a moment and watch these little guys. I'm curious about what you see."

They stood for some time in the rain and the wind, secure beneath the trees, mesmerized by the ants moving around and through the hive. Within minutes Jet gave witness to what Old Radar had shared earlier—she could recognize a division of labor with members of the colony, some worker-ants, some nurse-ants that care for the queen's eggs, some soldier-ants with special skills for defense and protection, and some builder-ants who seemed the most active in maintaining the structure of the colony during the storm.

Radar pointed out another team bringing food for everyone to share, leaving a scented trail behind them so others could continue to gather more from the prized area. Jet just stared at how coordinated it all seemed, but also just how random it appeared. At that very moment Radar whispered, "All of this is achieved without a complex language system, substituted by a very effective, universal, and basic mode of communication. That small amount of communication they share is always accurate, drives the right actions, and builds trust and cooperation throughout the entire colony. These guys learn from their mistakes and it's encouraged. Each ant has specific skills that match their talents, and together, with each trusting the other, the workplace thrives in perfect harmony." He paused, and added with a crooked smile, "It's not as *random* as you might think."

At that moment, Jet was unsure if she was more interested in the charm of ant-nirvana or how Old Radar seemed to know what she was thinking.

Soon enough they headed back to help Hummer. While making their way, Radar turned to Jet and said softly, "Jet, can I share something with you?"

"Sure."

"Hummer carries heavy pain from the losses caused by the expedition, and as hard as it may have been for you to hear him out about what occurred and how that all went down, I'm glad he found the strength to talk to you about it. He thinks the world of you, Jet, and it took courage and vulnerability on his part to share the regret he's carrying." He added, looking down while gently saying, "Regret like that can block the love, joy, and hope experiences we are all entitled to have during our earthly walk."

Before she could reply, Old Radar put his wing out to stop her. He pointed upward to a honeybee hive in the tree that must have been a foot wide and two feet long. "Check that out!" he said with a childlike glow about him.

Jet looked up, "The beehive?"

"Bees and ants have no direct connection, but they share similar qualities and complex ecosystems." He added, "Both successfully surviving, and thriving, on a global scale, for almost 100 million years. Like the ants, they communicate with a simple and basic language, but more effectively than most other species on the planet. Did you know humans have been bee-keeping the honeybee for almost 9,000 years? You would think they could learn a thing or two!" He laughed. "These here are honeybees, Jet."

"Why does this matter, Radar?"

"Jet, the honeybee contributes a ton to the overall biodiversity of our environment. By pollinating and cross-pollinating a variety of plants, many direct food sources are produced for other animals, and have tremendous impact on marine life, as well as humans.

"Yup, these little creatures are central to all we have and almost all we see! Even the branch I used to help the ants earlier today never would exist if not for these guys! It's all connected, Jet."

Continuing along the trail of wet leaves, with their distinct smell of Autumn mold, Jet circled the discussion back to Old Radar's comment about Hummer, while being sure they were far enough from the cove. "Radar, given our culture as a flock of geese, how we work together to protect one another, and seeing today how unruly, or random, nature can be, I can begin to understand that the events of last year were not anyone's fault." Her words faded off to a momentary silence, she added, "But my parents are gone, Radar—for whatever reason—and these days, I wish their ghosts would disappear as well."

Hummer was still sleeping as they entered the cove. The storm overhead moved more north.

That night Jet wrote again in her journal:

Thirty members flew inland to manage the storm, leaving us here. I just pray they are safe!

Ants, honeybees, and geese—so, we are all connected? Seems we are.

Learned a few things today:

> Nature empowers everyone to contribute, collaborate, and work together to overcome obstacles.

> Ants and bees adapt to their surroundings, never stuck in old ways.

> Each member has a role, no matter how small, impacting the whole team.

> We learn from mistakes. We move forward when we change.

She pondered those last few words
as she fell into a deep sleep.

CHAPTER 5

Each corner supports
the other, yet each side
also stands alone with
its own unique value.

The Triangle

E arly the next morning Radar took to the cloudy sky, surveying the storm and any damage left in its wake. Instantly, he found the skies clear, remnants of the storm still heading offshore to the Atlantic northeast. Surprisingly, very little water had surged into Boston Harbor. The damage was minimal. *We are good to go*, he thought to himself as he circled back to the cove.

Landing, he found Jet and Hummer awake, talking, and genuinely laughing together—about what he didn't care, just happy to see Jet's spirits high. He hesitated to interrupt. "The storm is now headed northeast, and the skies are clear to our south. We should head out soon if we are going to catch the flock."

Hummer strained to lift his voice, still not feeling a hundred percent, "I've been doing some thinking, some math, and mapped the fastest route we can take to meet up with everyone. Are you open to hearing my plan?"

Jet was a little shocked to be asked, given her lack of experience and seniority—but he was looking directly at her when he spoke. Radar showed interest and moved closer, delighted that Hummer was feeling better. Jet honked and let him know she was all ears!

"I suggest we head due south toward Long Island, just east of New York City, and stay over the eastern coastal waters. At Long Island, we cut inland and head west, flying just north of Philadelphia toward Hershey, Pennsylvania. We then pick up the Appalachian Trail running down the Eastern Continental Divide, following that south. If we stick together, get good updrafts, and hold our in-flight form, I think we can catch them in a day."

When Hummer finished there were no objections, just smiles all around. Jet took a breath and said, "If it's alright with you, I would like to lead us off today and take point." There was a sound of excitement in her voice.

Radar, witnessing Jet's willingness to lead, glanced over at Hummer with a smile. No words were spoken between them. Jet quickly took to the air, like a teenager heading out the door on a date, and they followed her into the sky, leaving Spot Pond behind—but grateful for the two days of refuge it had provided them.

Heading over Providence, Rhode Island, Radar calculated that their New York target was now almost 200 miles away, along the Atlantic coast. With Hummer unable to fly at top speed, he figured the group would take six hours to make it to Long Island.

Jet swapped up the drafting with Hummer every two hours, helping him to build his stamina and confidence—with Jet closing out the final stint of this leg by bringing them over the Long Island Sound toward Southampton. She led them down along Fire Island, deeper into the Great South Bay. She was following her instincts, having never been in the area. Eventually, Radar provided some direction and brought them to a stop in a small cove across from West Islip, along Gilgo State Park. *The place is teeming with wildlife*, thought Jet as she slid in next to Hummer, who was again looking weak and breathing more heavily from the long trip.

"Yes, this place is sure teeming with wildlife," Radar said. Jet spun her head back to look at Old Radar, given how his chosen words mirrored her own. He didn't blink. "I suggest we pause here for a few hours to rest up and eat. At nightfall, we exit and head southwest, north of Philadelphia, toward the Appalachian Trail, as planned," Radar added.

Hummer seemed too winded to speak, and Jet honked as she told Hummer to stay put while she flew off to explore the unknown, but infamous, Long Island Sound.

From the sky, Jet could see the storm damage caused by the hurricane two days earlier. Human power lines on Fire Island were down, trees snapped in half, and beaches torn up from the high winds and rough seas. But at the same time, she was overwhelmed with the abundance of shellfish and marine life all around her. A richness of life not seen in Quebec.

A pod of dolphins appeared below her, moving up the Sound as one. She followed them from above. They were working together to find food. The younger ones swam ahead and played in the waves, jumping three to four feet high and taking it in turns! This went on for some time as the adults, never far behind, worked together using biologically built-in sonar systems, known as *echolocation*, to navigate and locate food that, to Jet, seemed to be everywhere! She watched in awe as the pod, without hesitation, worked as a unit to herd prey by combining vocal clicks with synchronized swimming techniques. The communication was simple but highly effective. The dolphins seemed to be experts at corral-and-capture. Jet marveled from above as to how they showed a blend of art and science, working together through coordinated efforts with each other. Then they shared the meal, and the young fed equally on what was caught.

Jet found the entire process and coordinated approach almost overwhelming. She admired the mammals' teamwork, the different roles they played, and the abundance of trust they apparently shared. She thought about her own team and the amazing lessons from within her own flock; the drafting, the team-V formation, the honking, and so much more. She thought about the ant colony and the beehive and what Old Radar had pointed out back in Boston. But then suddenly the adult dolphins below her fanned out and gained tremendous speed to catch the young ones in front and began swirling around them, flapping their tails, circling around and around in a tight formation. From nowhere, a five-foot bull shark passed in the opposite direction.

Amazed, Jet almost fell out of the sky! She had heard her parents' stories about how dolphins will circle around and support the sick or a threatened smaller dolphin in danger, but she had never seen it in action. She had always thought the story of dolphins in New Zealand providing a protective circle for a young human surfer, until the great whites roaming the area departed, was nothing more than a tall tale. Now, here she was, on her first migration, witnessing all the collaborative power, trust, and intellect of this community from 30 feet above. She had never felt so inspired!

Suddenly, Old Radar slid in beside her, joining her in mid-air. "Pretty amazing, isn't it?" Jet was surprised he was able to find her and thought it was a little strange how Old Radar always seemed to just *show up*.

"Jet, we can learn a lot from the dolphin. Their communication and cooperation are critical for their survival in the ocean environment. Their complex social structures, strong family bonds, and effective communication methods enable them to work together efficiently, find food, avoid predators, and navigate the challenges of their marine habitats." Then he added, with purpose in his rough voice, "But more importantly today is how the dolphins demonstrated the finest living examples of Love and Joy."

"If the ants and the honeybees provide lessons of teamwork and our universal connection, the dolphins, with their intellect and social structure, help teach us the eternal source of true happiness."

He invited her to follow him and they landed on a deserted sandy beach at the southern tip of Fire Island, across from the mainland. Radar cleared an area with his foot. Grabbed a stick and drew a large, basic triangle in the sand.

Pointing down, he said, "Jet, the triangle is a symbol of strength, enlightenment, and spirituality found in many cultures and religions. From Christianity to Judaism to Buddhism, it shows up everywhere. It represents unity, perfection, and importance. Each corner supports the other, giving equal strength to all parts, yet each side also stands alone with its own unique value."

Wondering where he was going, Jet asked, "How does this relate to the dolphins or to," she paused, "to happiness?"

With a very intentional tone in his voice, he slowly stated, as if to pierce her outer shell, "It is also a symbol of enlightenment, allowing us to think and live beyond today."

Turning back to the sand, at the base of the triangle, he wrote one word in all capitals: LOVE. Along the left side he wrote JOY, and along the right of the triangle he wrote HOPE. Jet stood and watched as Old Radar performed his rudimentary artwork on the beach.

When he finished, he said, "Jet, the triangle of Love, Hope, and Joy is central to all meaning of life on earth. Having, and sometimes just finding, a balance with these three elements, principles if you will, is the essence of true happiness. Here, the adage of 'it's about the journey, not the destination' really takes meaning."

He looked up at her, lifting his strong head, "All creatures survive and find meaning using any combination of these three principles. Great leaders understand these elements the most. But you must know what you are looking for to truly witness it. Today the dolphins showed you two of these, demonstrating both Love and Joy. The Joy of the pod, of family, of community, is mixed with a childlike play. With Joy, and through Joy, we bring forth our inner light and we shine outwardly, we journey on earth with purpose. You saw that with the flow of the dolphins in the sound—how they radiated unity, hunting efficiently, playing authentically, and working together in friendship and purpose, all as an absolute act of togetherness and of sharing. True Joy is never singular, or separating, but is found in the collective of *we*." He paused, still looking down, "*Jet, Joy is our we.*"

He continued, knowing he had her attention, "The other example you saw today was Love, another side of the same triangle. Some say it anchors the triangle and feeds the other two sides. Others say that Love receives Joy and Hope from the opposing sides at each connecting vertex," pointing to its corners for Jet to understand. He continued, "Love is then completed by these two sides, as we are. Either way, the tenet of Love in our lives must be seen as a blessing and is very meaningful within the context of our own total happiness." At his feet, he slowly drew a circle around the word *Love*.

"When the adult dolphins provided the protective circle around their youth, that was Love. An action based on a willingness to do for others what is right, even if it involves risk. It's more complicated than this, but, put simply, *Love is family*." He looked up to see Jet just staring at him, her eyes moving back and forth from the triangle in the sand to him, while they slowly filled with tears.

"You're saying my parents loved me," her voice firm and reflective. The words burst out of her. She paused as Radar stood silently waiting for her to speak again. "And that I should cherish the love they gave me, even if they are not here," she caught her breath, finding it difficult to speak through the pain, "because if the roles were reversed, I too would have put *we* first and jumped at the same damn expedition they took, doing what is right for the wider flock." She emphasized *we*. She stared silently at the triangle a while longer, circling around Old Radar to observe the three-sided shape from his perspective, a sense of peace and awakening coming into her heart as she took each small step.

Wiping away her tears, "Okay, so how does Hope come into it?"

"Good question," he said, pointing his stick to the word *Hope*. "This is the side of the triangle that requires the most effort from all of us, like sweat and sometimes heartache.

Hope is a verb in this context. It's action! This is where Love and Joy go to work by taking the gifts of light, happiness, and divine providence, which reside within us, and combine them for others to bring Hope to those we touch and encounter. When all three come together, we live in balance with our own triangle, with Hope drawing others in, like bees to the honey or a moth to the light. We rise by lifting others through our Hope, and, well, we are then living to our fullest potential helping others find theirs." He paused and looked up at Jet. "The world has always needed Hope, and it takes individuals like you, Jet, to bring such Hope to others."

He slowly traced the entire triangle with the stick, "When you bundle Love and Joy you naturally inspire Hope in others and help others find *balance* within their *own triangle.* Then the process starts all over again, like lighting another candle. Love, Hope and Joy are eternal, Jet, and the greatest of these is Love."

In that moment, Jet realized that Old Radar was again referring to her parents. That her own parents provided her with an example of this eternal gift. It was always there. She realized in that very moment that she could either ignore what had been demonstrated to her in their time together, failing to find happiness and failing to bring her own gifts forward, or she could act on it, living in a way they would be proud, igniting Hope, and keeping the eternal process alive.

With Jet deep in thought, Radar witnessed his lesson had landed and had its intended effect. He gave it a few moments before he broke the silence, "Hey, are you aware how Hummer got his nickname?"

Jet snapped back to the present, a little off balance from all she discovered in the last hour or so. "Hummer is his nickname? Everyone just knows him as Hummer."

"It's Thomas. Ever since he was a young boy, Thomas hummed when he was happy. Unaware of his own habit, or that he was disturbing the peace around him, he would just hum. I'm told he hummed a lot."

Jet chuckled at the thought, and Radar joined her, "Kind of funny, right?" Then, he said, "Have you heard him humming, lately?"

Jet said flatly, "Nope!"

Tossing aside the stick he used to draw the triangle and facing her as she continued to stare at the sand, "There's a reason he doesn't hum anymore. He's lost his balance, his inner light faded from him, and his own triangle is almost broken; that failed expedition last year took away his Joy. Right or wrong, his Hope for redemption, or maybe just recovery, is now placed in you, Jet. But let me be clear, there was a time Hummer could light up a room with his internal glow."

Jet's mind churned like the storm that passed overhead two nights earlier. A myriad of questions, of anger, love for her lost parents, nature and its connective tissue, of ants and honeybees in perfect symphony, the dolphins' performance to serve and protect each other, the triangle of purpose and happiness—all swirling within her. She thought about her role in the flock. She felt confused and speechless by the many unexpected lessons from a gander who seemed old enough to be her father. Old Radar had made an impact on her in a short space of time, and she knew it! She finally turned to him, a little exhausted, and simply said, "C'mon. Let's go check on Hummer, it's getting late."

They found him resting, seemingly more prepared for this next leg of the migration, the long, westward flight inland. Jet noticed bags under Hummer's eyes and slipped away to journal, keen to capture all that hit her while on Fire Island:

Letting go is how I will move forward.

When we act selflessly for the good of others, we are all a living example of love, hope, and joy.

> Love = Family and connection.
Love is the base for Hope and Joy.

> Hope = A verb. It's what we transmit to others through our loving and joyful actions.

> Joy = Our gifted purpose and where we shine the most.

Each supports the other. The three sides work together.

Living in purpose to balance our triangle produces a path to happiness that is eternal. It's a journey, not a destination.

CHAPTER 6

All good leaders
sacrifice first.

Hummer and the Cherokee Elder

At 11 p.m. they exited Long Island Sound flying west and expecting headwinds from the northerly currents. While working hard at the front of the formation, Jet was thankful she could set a strong pace, becoming internally aware of her hope as she looked forward to reuniting with the flock.

In short order, she heard Hummer breathing heavily behind her and wondered if he was up to the demand of the many overnight miles ahead. *But he seems to be keeping pace,* she thought to herself, still wondering about the comments Old Radar shared regarding "all the hope" Hummer placed in her.

Another two hours passed, and the geese honked to adjust positions once again.

Flying for over six hours, covering great distance, the rugged Pennsylvania terrain was finally beginning to light up, filled with early morning sun. Trees along the mountain ranges of the Appalachians stood tall. As each minute passed, they enjoyed an ever-increasing glow of the foliage below, bringing to life bright red, yellow, burnt white, and orange leaves while slowly giving life to the entire mountain range and its spectacular patchwork of vibrant fall color. Adding to the beauty was a very thin and low hanging set of clouds nestled within the foothills. From a few thousand feet above, it looked like cotton gently threading together the trees, the mountains, and the colors. Gliding above, Jet thought of Old Radar's earlier teaching that "everything is connected," and from her perspective of this masterpiece below her, she knew she would never argue on this point.

They flew on in awe of the rich, natural beauty filled with its indescribable colors. Jet was about to share how the Appalachian Mountains look like small, magical hills from their altitude, but right on cue, as if reading her mind, Radar announced, "And far off to the east of these magical foothills, at about 220 miles, is the tip of the Chesapeake Bay." Growing accustomed to Old Radar's telepathic ways, Jet just stared out to her left trying to find the watershed as she drafted off Hummer, now leading the group.

"At this pace, we might be in Georgia sometime tomorrow," Hummer coughed—then honked to show he was still up to leading for a little longer.

Seconds later, *boom!* A loud crack filled the air. Then another cracking explosion—the intense sound bouncing up from the mountain walls was deafening. Jet's ears were ringing. She was disoriented and suddenly thrown from her flight path.

"Move!" shouted Radar.

Hummer was already veering from his position in the team and swinging below. He left his position in front of Jet and flew with all his might, honking.

"What's he doing?" Jet barked. Her eyes bulged with fear as her heart raced. She couldn't think. The thundering cracks continued to ring out.

"He's protecting! It's what the leader does when there is danger or a predator is in the area—the ultimate in servant leadership—they lead, no matter the consequence. It's instinct." Radar watched with intensity yet was also puzzled by the sudden events.

The echoing booms were coming from the trees below. Hummer's efforts seemed to be working, but suddenly it seemed he had become a target for the humans and their strange lead-filled barrels. Although straining for speed against the wind, he was almost 500 yards away and the thundering sounds seemed to have vanished. Then, one final blast, and Hummer's feathers suddenly exploded. He dropped from the sky, falling without effort or resistance. His long neck and bright beak held high above his body, looking up to the clouds as he fell, his long wings went limp as he plummeted. Hummer's fall took almost seven seconds, then he was gone from sight, disappearing into the tall forest. To Radar and Jet, these seven seconds seemed like *forever*. Hummer was dead before he ever hit the ground.

"Nooooooo!" Jet cried out. She watched as the humans below release their dogs to fetch their prize: setting out to collect Hummer.

"Keep moving, Jet. We need to keep moving." On instinct, Radar separated from Jet to make it harder for the humans below. They banked right, about 25 yards apart from one another, dropping below the tree line, safer from becoming a target. They could hear the barking. The marsh, however, as thick and wet from the heavy storm making it impossible for the dogs to do their job. Just then, another explosion and the buckshot pellets flew past them. "Nothing more we can do, Jet, let's go."

After some time to process the horror she just experienced, Jet turned and asked, "Why would Hummer bring us this way, Radar, if he knew it was dangerous? And why did he fly ahead at the sound of hunters?" Jet begged for the answer as she looked at Old Radar with tears in her eyes. The loss of Hummer was too much and almost unbearable.

"Jet, part of me supposes Hummer thought he wasn't going to make it all the way to Tampa. He was very sick, and he knew it. But to answer your question, he flew ahead of us to become a target and to distract the hunters below. Once they focused on him, he knew you would have a good chance to pass over without much risk. This area is filled with weekend warriors and their rifles. Hummer knew what he was doing. He brought us this way because he knew it was the only way to catch and reconnect with the flock, even if it meant the risk of the October game hunters."

Radar paused a few moments.

"Jet, I know this is hard right now. Nobody starts a journey to not finish it, and nobody starts a relationship for it to end, but it happens.

"Endings are not always as they appear, Jet. They are never just endings, there is always another side to things. It's hard to see this right now, I get that, but an ending often becomes a new beginning as well." Radar then, in a low voice, added, "As you grow into the Jet you will one day become, you will better understand the decision and the sacrifice Hummer made here. His leadership matters, so too his actions to support the broader goal of the flock. Not to take such evasive moves at the sound of danger would have been against his genetic makeup, not to mention his role as a leader in the flock. All good leaders sacrifice first. His leadership was not just a job, it's a calling to serve others." He paused, giving thought to what he wanted to share next with her. "Jet, we can't change the events of today and we can't bring Hummer back. All we can do is work together to complete the journey he sacrificed himself for, working together to honor Hummer."

The two flew on for some time without talking, both processing the ultimate act of self-sacrifice displayed by Hummer earlier that day. Both angry and in awe of him at the same time.

"Maybe Hummer could have made it," Jet said, more of a question than a statement. "Maybe we could have helped him through his own personal storm? Maybe I could have really been his hope?"

"Maybe. You do have what it takes, Jet." He cleared his throat, "I think Hummer's been very sick for some time and this trip was taking its toll on him. But still, sickness or not, it doesn't change his actions today—it was instinct he followed. Leadership, anchored in love, to the very end."

Jet tried to stay positive. "And you had just drawn the triangle while we were at Fire Island!" Radar could feel the impact on Jet. Then she said, as if thinking out loud, "Hummer was clever, so he must have had good reason to choose us to be on his team. But why? What do you and I have that would see him choose us to partner with? Why us? Why me?"

They stopped for the day, a little off course due to the chaos, resting on the most southern tip of Deep Creek Lake, Maryland. The sun set over the mountains as they slid onto the calm water. The sky was lit up with a now familiar orange glow, sharply cut by the shaded mountains, west of the lake. The bright orange glow stretched upward forever in such a way that it almost seemed as if Hummer had called it up himself to say all is well. The silence on the lake and the bright orange glow above almost brought Jet to tears.

Finally, Radar blurted, "Jet, you're right!" With a quickened pace to his growly voice he said, "Hummer chose his team with good reason. And if I were to guess, you bring a strength of character and a remarkable level of determination. You can walk through walls, and nothing will stop you once you get an idea in your head. He knew he needed that on his team."

He slowed down, thinking a little longer. "For me, well, I think I bring some experience, albeit weathered these days," he chuckled to himself. "I've been down every southern passage Canadian geese can take from Quebec." Looking off mid-distance as if recalling images from his past, he then added, "Rookie, I've seen every darn weather pattern the universe can put in front of us."

"I'm just happy you're still here to talk about it," Jet smiled at her old friend.

Radar didn't respond to her smiling comment.

"Hummer needed you on a few levels, for your talents and strength, but also for abilities that you may not yet realize you possess." Almost a full minute of silence passed, then Radar spoke with real purpose in his voice, "Jet, I think Hummer knew something like this might happen and maybe we've been brought together to balance each other in ways that provide the best chance of you finishing this journey without him."

Working hard to put aside the pain from the day, Jet grew more curious. She looked at Old Radar hoping he would continue.

"I'm certain he saw in you the gifts God placed in your hands. The good Lord knows you are filled with a passion for good, while also possessing all the tools of a budding leader. As I said on the beach at Fire Island, I think you became the target of Hummer's Hope. I bet it's why he insisted you joined the migration, put you on his team, and why he's been letting you lead in flight so often. He's been getting you out of your comfort zone, empowering you, and preparing you. He wants you to step up!"

Jet sat on the lake looking toward the shaded mountainside, the orange glow now a dusty pink and almost gone with a fast-setting sun. She was unsure how to process what Old Radar was sharing. She felt Hummer's loss. Inside she admitted to herself she was a little scared and confused by it all.

"Do you think we can make it, just the two of us?"

"We will need to work together if we are going to make up the time and catch the flock. I know the way, but you are going to have to trust me. Don't be scared, Jet—the universe has you right where you are meant to be."

With just the two of them on the lake, off-course, and hundreds of miles from the flock, Jet suddenly felt the full loss of Hummer. Unexpected images of her parents flooded her, bringing back dark feelings she was working to leave behind. She felt alone sitting on the lake, even with Radar by her side. She struggled to understand her role in the flock and all of the events over the last few days. She slowly closed her eyes and took a deep breath, searching for clues.

Radar gently added, "Jet, I hope by the time we get to Tampa you recognize just how important your role is within the wider flock, and how ready you are for your next chapter, even if you don't think you are."

"I don't know what to think."

"Jet, all forms of personal growth require internal work. We adjust when we are invited to let go of parts of our past to make room for what's to come." He added, without moving or opening his eyes to speak, "Remember, Jet, everything is connected, and our own thoughts can disempower us if they are negative. When we use negativity to process what happens to us, it becomes our anchor, holding us back from ever being what we are capable of being. Negativity blocks our natural light."

They both rested in silence for some time.

Using the sunlight's final moments, Jet reached for her journal, hoping to soften the events of the day and helping her to bring some order it all:

Goodbye Hummer! Hello "whatever."
Change is constant! Every ending
brings new beginnings.

All good leaders sacrifice first.
When done well, it's done with Love.

Leading serves others. But
remember, a true leader is focused
on the team and the mission, not
on title, or power, or self-appointed
rule.

It was dark when she finished her words and the world around her was calm and silent, including Old Radar, or so she thought.

"Even our arrival on this lake, resting here in the mountains, on the very eastern edge of the once great Cherokee Nation is no coincidence, Jet," he said in a very low, sleepy, voice—startling Jet.

He paused. Only the sound of crickets and bullfrogs could now be heard. "Perhaps the Tale of Two Wolves, which is an old Cherokee lesson, will speak to those swirling internal emotions and all that sorrow you feel inside? Jet, you must leave behind what holds you back."

Jet turned in the water to listen to the tale, taking in the sea of stars above as Old Radar shared his story.

> One evening an elder in the Cherokee tribe told his grandson about a battle that goes on inside us. He said, "My son, the battle is between two '*wolves*' inside each of us.
>
> "One is Evil. It is anger, envy, regret, doubt, jealousy, sorrow, greed, arrogance, self-pity, guilt, resentment, inferiority, lies, false pride, superiority, and ego.
>
> "The other is Good. It is joy, hope, love, peace, serenity, humility kindness, compassion, empathy, generosity, gratefulness, forgiveness, truth, and faith."

The grandson thought about the two wolves for a moment and then asked his grandfather: "*Which wolf wins?*"

The Cherokee elder simply replied, "*The one you feed.*" —Author unknown

CHAPTER 7

Through my word
and my action
an example to the flock,

I feel up to the task,
with you as my rock.

The Dream

That night, Jet dreamt. It was a strong and transformative dream, filled with incredible color, honest conversation, enjoyment, and the sounds of happiness that seemed to come from her past, her present, and her future. Time seemed to collapse and fold in on itself, as if it was happening in real time, yet happening in a parallel dimension. Her dream felt like she was lost inside forever, yet time also encircled her as if nothing mattered but the now. Time and dimension lost all meaning and measure. She didn't know where she was, but she knew exactly where she was.

She found herself at an elaborately set dining table with her parents. A majestic table adorned with a soft white linen tablecloth, peppered with dozens of tall, lit candelabras. Heavy silverware was laid out at the place settings, suggesting multiple courses. Gold etched saucers perfectly placed in front of each chair. She was the invited guest at this table, her parents the hosts. A younger version of Radar was there, serving them all in perfect form and in a very formal fashion. The room glowed in a way she had never seen but had always known.

When the meal finished and the candles had burned low, following an eternity of discussion, her parents came to her and wrapped themselves around her, hugging her as only parents can. It lasted forever and she was touched by a kiss.

Just then, she awoke unexpectedly in the middle of the lake surrounded by an early morning mist coming off the still waters of Deep Creek. Bewildered, Jet was surprised to find it was all but a dream—yet the details of the room, the glow, the food, and the final hug, all so vivid! She stayed there for some time, in the quiet of the morning, enjoying the dream sensation and relishing an inner warmth she had not felt since she was little.

Slowly, as the sun reached above the hills, bringing daylight back into the colorful trees, the rays burned away the mist that blanketed her. Jet reached for her journal, drawn by her dream. The words from her heart fell rapidly onto the pages. She didn't stop writing, she didn't pause, nor overthink the state of "flow" she was experiencing. She wrote and wrote in a way that she never had, being pulled by a force she had never felt. Feeling more alive than ever, her pages filled with words, thoughts, and ideas. Then a poem formed.

Someday is coming,
it's coming, I know.
To thank you both,
for helping me grow.

You've made my eyes smile,
and you've made them cry,
I feel you're still with me,
but I can't explain why.

Your love is everlasting,
rising up in need.
Bringing hope and joy,
these are blessings indeed.

And when that someday comes,
it'll reveal all worth.
'Cause that someday is coming!
it's been coming since birth.

But there is work to do,
you say for me.
Bringing love, hope, and joy
for others to see.

Through my word and my action
an example to the flock,
I feel up to the task.
with you as my rock.

The love in me now,
is a feeling I've known.
From the day I was born,
to the dream just shown.

I know you're still with me,
I just can't explain how.
Please come back in my dreams,
don't go, not now.

When she finished her heart was pounding as she looked back over the words. Overwhelmed by the intense experience of being with her parents again, she was filled with a wellspring of emotion. Out of nowhere she began to weep joyfully in the peaceful morning sunshine reflecting off the lake. She moved to the top of her raw poem, titling it, "Someday."

CHAPTER 7.5

"Happiness is when what you think, what you say, and what you do are in harmony."

—Mahatma Gandhi

A Perpetual Triangle

*"Happiness is when what you think, what you say, and
what you do are in harmony."* —Mahatma Gandhi

The triangle is a geometric shape with a rich history and a set of unique strengths that make it a fundamental concept in mathematics, science, art, and religion. The concept of the triangle appears in mathematical texts from Egypt and Babylon, dating back as early as 1900 BC.

The ancient Greeks made significant contributions to the study of triangles, with mathematicians like Euclid exploring their properties in detail. Euclid's *Elements* is one of the most influential mathematical works of all time, and it contains extensive discussions of triangles and their properties. Throughout history various cultures used the triangle as symbols of **strength, stability, and balance.** Christianity, Buddhism, and Hinduism all apply the triangle in various ways to offer a framework for meaning and enlightenment.

The strength of the triangle is in its simplicity. It is a basic, two-dimensional shape characterized by three sides and three angles. This simplicity makes it an essential building block, able to be applied to various domains. In geometry and trigonometry, the triangle is used to understand angles and the relationships between angles and sides. In engineering and architecture, triangles provide stability and support in structures like trusses and pyramids. The triangle is essentially considered the most rigid, sturdy, and weight-bearing shape known to mankind. Examples of applications anchored in the triangle are found throughout physics, navigation, and engineering.

In more recent times, various offensive and defensive sporting schemes use the triangle to drive winning constructs, leveraging play from three different, but rotating, positions.

This fundamental geometric shape is storied for its strength, harmony, and balance in cultures, works, and philosophy. Its simplicity helps promote equilibrium and brings enduring relevance. **When created in balance, it is perpetual.**

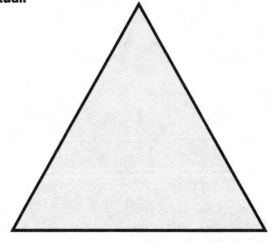

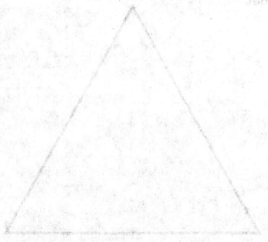

CHAPTER 8

Like a waiter at a fine dining table, I find Joy by serving others.

What's in a Name

L ater that day, as the two headed due south, along the Continental Divide, high above the Blue Ridge Mountains, Deep Creek Lake now far behind them, Jet remained contemplative about her dream. How tangible and real it all felt. She relished the final hug with her parents just before she awoke.

As they flew on, she felt an urge to know more about Old Radar, the waiter in her dramatic dream. That crusty, kind, weathered elder who, for some reason, wanted to share his stories and life lessons with her.

Continuing to enjoy the kaleidoscope of brilliant color of autumn leaves below while they glided south along the updrafts from the mountains, she asked, "I just know you as Radar, but where does that come from?"

Old Radar took his time to answer. Jet was accustomed to this since they left Quebec.

"It seems my name evolved from a pattern of experiences others had through me," he offered in a flat, but low tone, looking off into the distance as if remembering parts of his past.

"Experiences *through you*? I'm not tracking, what does that mean?" Jet shot back, naturally curious.

"Well, we've already discussed how we are all born with certain gifts, Jet. But everyone is different! And without over complicating it, everyone's journey on earth is to discover purpose and meaning and to use the gifts granted to them at birth." He went on, "In the animal kingdom, this happens more naturally. Take the ants, for example. They know from the moment they hatch what their role is within the colony, and they never doubt their God-given talents. Like the honeybee, they don't have to think about it. Some are workers with the strength to carry fifty times their own weight, some are carers of the queen's eggs, while others are protectors of the nest, born with speed, a longer reach, and keen skills of observation." He paused a moment.

Jet looked at him with one eye, curious and a little confused as to where he was heading with this, but she was open to learning and continued to listen.

"As you move up the hierarchy in the animal kingdom, say, all the way up to humans, it becomes more difficult to understand your innate gifts and talents. We bump into the complications of life, we chase false hopes, and we deal with emotional factors that take us off course from what brings us the most purpose and happiness. So many spend years, even decades, feeling confused or unfulfilled—always searching. The higher you go in our hierarchy, the hazier it is and the harder it is to find your true *playground*." Before she could say anything, he quickly added, "And while humans are the worst at detecting their own true gifts and talents, the gaggle is not far behind."

"What does this have to do with how you got your nickname?"

"Jet, it seems my gift is to help others find theirs. Along the way, the name Radar evolved as I went about my earthly walk. Today, given my years, it evolved into Old Radar," he said with a chuckle, glancing back at her with the same one-eye look she gave him earlier.

Jet blushed, then smiled and kindly offered, "I think the name suits you!" She felt caught out.

"So how do we ever know if we've uncovered our God-given gifts and talents, and how long does all *that* take?" she asked, emphasizing the word *that*. Without pausing, she added, "And how do you know if your gift actually works to impact others as intended?"

"Great questions, Jet!" Old Radar took a moment to consider his reply. "Well," he said, "in fact, these are the most important questions of all. Discovering the answers to these questions brings life to your triangle.

"You know you are in your *playground* when you feel fulfilled and at peace with the amount Love, Hope, and Joy you are experiencing in your life and with those around you. There becomes a natural balance between *who you are* and *what you do* in your day-to-day and within the community.

I call this place *your playground* because everyone can remember how easy, happy, and free they were as a youngster on the playground. You knew where you fit, you didn't need permission to act, and you knew the system allowed you to be you—to be free. Sadly, as we age, we reserve these feelings to the youth and convince ourselves that this feeling of freedom doesn't extend beyond the playground."

"Okay. So we know we are in balance with our gifts and talents when we feel this sense of 'freedom' within—is that what you're saying?" Jet asked.

"It's not as easy as that, but essentially, yes, *freedom* is the best word to describe what I'm trying to get at, but we could replace that with *ease* or *autonomy*. It's when the work we do is no longer work, and our efforts form part of a bigger system at play and a system that we feel connected to." He added, recognizing Jet was taking it all in, "It's like your whole life has become your playground."

"And we are one with our gifts and talents, just as you drew on the sand at Fire Island, balancing Love, Hope, and Joy," Jet offered up as if thinking out loud and finishing his sentence.

"Correct!" said Old Radar.

They flew on, silently, Radar letting Jet internalize the idea of her playground. Then Jet asked, "So, does everyone find their true gifts and talents? Does everyone discover their *playground?*" Jet asked. The mountains of North Carolina

were rising up to 5,000 feet as they approached, instinc-
tively increasing their altitude to be at a safer distance from
possible hunters.

"Perhaps I can answer that through an anonymous parable, written and passed on many years ago, that's been
retold a number of times, Jet."

> A good man dies and his soul floats upward.
> He finds St. Peter standing in front of a group,
> addressing them. The good man realizes they
> are about to go on a tour—a welcome tour, if you
> will, and he joins the group at the back.
>
> St. Peter is explaining to the group the entire
> area and how things work. Pointing to gathering
> areas, practice areas, where certain souls have
> special access, and so forth. Off to the left is a
> very large, dark-gray warehouse building Peter
> failed to mention. The man finds this strange and
> interrupts the tour, asking, "What is that building
> used for?"
>
> St. Peter says, "That is the only area off-limits
> and is forbidden to visit up here." With that, he
> moves on with the tour.
>
> But the man is not satisfied; he thinks to himself,
> *Off-limits? How can eternity have off-limits?* Curi-
> osity gets the better of him, and he considers his
> next action without risk. Around the next cloud

he spins off and away from the group and heads to the massive gray structure. He kicks in the small access door and enters.

Looking up, he finds he is in a massive warehouse with rows and rows of standing shelves, aisle after aisle, as far as the eye can see. On each shelf, with just one inch separating them, are bright, white boxes, the size of a shoebox. Wrapped around each white box is a red ribbon—as red as he's ever seen, with a tied bow at the top. On each box is a name, printed in small black type, last name first. He also notices that the boxes are in alphabetical order.

The man tears down the aisle looking for the box with his name. Finding his very own box, he climbs up to pull it down. Untying the bright red bow, he tears off the ribbon and removes the lid.

Looking inside the box for a moment or two, the man lets out a long, sad, guttural cry and falls to his knees as he stares intently inside his box.

Suddenly, the door he entered through opens again and St. Peter is walking down the hall toward the crying man: arms outstretched to console the weeping visitor.

Shadows from the group following the tour guide fall along the warehouse floor from the sunlight now washing in through the open door.

St. Peter has his hand on the sobbing man's shoulder when a voice from the group asks, "So, what's in the box?"

The saint turns to the group and says, "In the box are all the gifts and all the talents that the universe gave you from birth that you never discovered, you never used during your lifetime, which, if discovered by you, would bring you an abundance of love, hope, and joy—beyond measure."

—Author unknown

Radar paused, adding, "Jet, I help people discover what's in their box. To find their *playground* and their true balance. But it doesn't mean everyone accepts the offer or seizes the opportunity to live aligned with such a purpose. Every life is a unique journey, and we all have choices. Sadly, many never discover what is available to them, are unaware of their choice, or worse, they're aware and refuse to act, being held back by a form of fear or the Evil Wolf."

Jet flew in silence for a long while. Radar gave her time to think, then she said, "Cool story, Radar. Thanks for sharing that!"

"You bet, Jet. Like a waiter at a fine dining table, I find Joy by serving others. And I hope that parable helped you— even if it is a long-winded way to explain my nickname," he joked.

Jet was stunned by his word choice and the phrasing, *like a waiter at a fine dining table*. But before she could say anything about her dream, their destination appeared over the hills—beautiful Lake Toxaway in North Carolina. Old Radar targeted this lake to stop for the night, a halfway marker between Deep Creek Lake in Maryland and the Tampa Bay area. A lake safe from hunters.

"Approximately 500 miles south, with 500 miles to go!" Old Radar said as he swooped down from the sky toward the center of the lake. Jet followed closely behind. Both geese were almost blinded by the brightness of the changing leaves surrounding the entire lake: red, yellow, orange, mixed with soft greens and brown; some tumbled onto the water in the gentle breeze. The 360-degree reflection of color on the lake during sunset made their landing breathtaking.

They pulled up directly in front of the Greystone Inn, a lodge for humans that dated back over 100 years. Old Radar had a dozen stories to share about the place and more stories of how he learned of this lake from all his travels. Jet was tired from the journey and began to drift off. She, however, wanted to journal all that she was experiencing.

The poem was her last journal work, now playing in her mind as she fought to stay awake. She felt the love from her parents again dial up inside her. This time she noticed a deeper reaction within, as if her soul was connecting the dots set down earlier in the day from Old Radar and anchoring on his triangle in the sand. This feeling carried a deep truth along with a sense of eternity that she had never felt before.

Overwhelmed, yet feeling safely protected for the first time in almost a year, she reached for her journal, begged Old Radar's pardon, and moved away. She poured out what was going on inside:

We all have gifts and talents, and everyone's purpose on earth is to discover their playground.

Our purpose is not found in a job, but aligned in belief that our life is part of a greater whole, and our gifts and talents matter.

Our playground is the place where we are living in balance with our love, hope, and joy—where we feel balanced and free.

when we live aligned to our purpose, we live in balance with the triangle of Love, Hope, and Joy.

Feed the right wolf.

CHAPTER 9

Your future is bigger
than your past.

The Samurai

The final leg of their journey to Tampa Bay, Florida, was here! As Jet rose, she found herself in a deep and contemplative state. With Old Radar still sleeping, Jet relished cool morning air, the backdrop of the old Inn, and some quiet time.

She pulled out her journal to reflect on all she had been writing and to revisit all that had occurred since they left Quebec in such chaotic fashion. She bristled reading her early words from the start, "*I hate this! And I hate them! Why do I need to go to Tampa? I DON'T NEED ANYONE ELSE! I prefer being alone, why can't they see that?*" So much inside her had changed since then, she thought.

Turning the pages, she quietly laughed out loud, in spite of herself, at how quickly she embraced her true gaggle-culture. The organized chaos when takeoff and landing, the history and the effectiveness behind the "honk," and the benefit of total vision for all members, the importance of team clarity to reach a destination, and the enhanced flying distance produced from the team-V formation that geese use when traveling together. *This is my family*, she realized.

She thought about the ant colony, the honeybees, and the dolphins, each different, yet each connected through a shared ecosystem. She smiled recalling Old Radar's words in her head, "*Everything is connected.*" She paused to reflect on how each species deploys their own, equally high-level, quality verbal and non-verbal communication methods. Jet marveled at the idea that nature enables interaction and communication strategies such as territory marking, food gathering, conflict resolution, and refining role clarity through clicks, dances, head movements, and even honks, to achieve the team mission. To her it just seemed so simple that each member relied on the other through a deeply embedded culture of trust to get the job done—working together inside equally complex social systems to thrive. She marveled at her notes from Fire Island and reflected on the triangle crudely drawn in the sand, a shape now etched permanently in her mind. She redrew the image in her journal while resting in the morning mist of Lake Toxaway.

When she finished, she felt mindful and was called to admit to herself that standing on that deserted shore on Long Island Sound, she quietly began to adore Old Radar as he unpacked Love, Hope, and Joy, gently showing her that she obtained these gifts and principles from her parents. This eternal offering presented in the shape of the triangle deeply resonated with her, and in this moment on the lake, she recognized her playground was calling her. She had never felt so inspired.

Turning the pages, she slowly teared up at the poetry that had fallen from her heart after the intense dream she experienced in Deep Creek, the same day she lost Hummer to the humans' game of hunting. She read it again and again, feeling within the same mystic swirl traveling through her mind, body, and soul, as she moved through the stanzas.

She blinked back her tears, caught her breath, looked up to the heavens, and whispered, "Thank you" to her parents. Then she turned the page again.

Finally, she came across her notes from Old Radar's parable about discovering one's own internal gifts and talents. *Gifts, when found and acted upon, bring even more meaning, more agency, and more purpose to the universal principles of Love, Hope, and Joy. The intersection of all three is where our playground lives*, she could hear him saying.

She closed her scruffy and traveled journal. A feeling of reconciliation came over her. She noticed in that moment she was calmer than she had felt for some time. *What an epic journey this has been*, she thought. There was a sense of excitement insider her. But yet, deep inside things were not fully *balanced*. She chuckled to herself for using Old Radar's language. She missed Hummer—a good gander working through his own demons who sacrificed through his leadership and who had put his Hope in her. She missed him and began wondering how best to honor him once they reached Tampa. She missed her parents too, still holding some hurt from their sudden loss. Somehow, however, their ghosts seemed more welcome. Old Radar had exposed her to the universal laws of Love and the ways of personal change, and she could feel them at work in her.

She knew she was unfolding from the person she was in Quebec. Lifting her head again, looking to the sky, she understood, deep in her bones, that their intense Love was eternal and capable of propelling her forward, never holding her back. But Jet also had a small part of her resisting the transformation taking place over the last few days. It was all so much, and she seemed unsure just how to bring it all together, how to completely let go of all the hurt brought about by this insufferable feeling of loss she carried deep inside.

Moments later Old Radar rose and without much discussion, they lifted off from Lake Toxaway heading south for their final miles.

"This final leg will take us hours, Jet," Radar said as they reached almost 11,000 feet, just high enough above the Blue Ridge Mountains to obtain a good perspective on their path down the remaining part of the Appalachian Trail. The lake itself rested at 4,000 feet above sea level. "We remain due-south almost the entire way. But the winds in these areas are often unfavorable, currents from the Gulf Stream don't allow us to fly at top speed the closer we get to Florida. But maintaining an average clip of 40 to 50 miles per hour, we should be in Tampa before sunset."

"We got this," Jet replied, a tinge of excitement in her voice. She was happy to be in the air. Radar took a deep breath and locked in behind her to draft whatever he could, inwardly satisfied with her renewed spirit over the last few days.

After two hours, the Appalachian Trail closed out at Springer Mountain, Georgia, and Old Radar navigated the remaining hours using landmarks he mapped from earlier migrations. They cruised south, heading away from Atlanta, toward Athens, Georgia, before banking right again toward Macon. "From here we will follow the human trail and stay above the wheels on Route 75 until we get to Florida," Old Radar said, breaking the silence, as the birds had found their rhythm and worked in sync to cover many miles in swift time.

Jet was happy to have the uninterrupted time to think. She didn't reply. Old Radar could sense she was processing her development over this migration and provided her with the needed space.

Eventually they approached Gainesville, Florida, with the sunshine now burning on them from the west and the air temperature now intensely different from the early morning conditions of Lake Toxaway. Radar knew the journey was about to end soon and dropped back a little to fly adjacent to Jet. "Before we get to Tampa, I want to thank you for being on my team. I've enjoyed flying with you, Jet. I can see why Hummer put such Hope in you! Your future is bigger than your past."

Jet looked at Old Radar and didn't say anything at first. She pondered those words—*your future is bigger than your past*. They just flew together. Besides, she had become unaccustomed to compliments over the last year, hiding away alone so often. After a few minutes, she asked, "How do I do this, Radar? How do I bring my triangle of Love, Hope, and Joy to life when I know I still carry some sorrow...maybe even a little anger?"

Old Radar honked and then nudged her to bank right, keeping her on course toward Tampa. He then said, "Your own heart will guide you, Jet. The anger you feel is born from a sorrow you carry with you—a sorrow I'm detecting is slowly transforming ever since we left Quebec. This is good! Jet, you have experienced loss. We all suffer loss in our lives; it is part of the journey. Reframing the loss is a transformation that will set you free. Loss feeds sorrow when we let it dwell. Letting go of the loss, which has fed your sorrow, will also remove any emotions of anger. We start by simply recognizing the emotions and being grateful for changes, even if they are small." He paused to let her take in the depth of his message.

"Jet, the choice to hold on to loss—or to let go of that loss—is just that, it's a choice. And when the universal pull of Love, Hope, and Joy spark an awareness of your gifts and talents to serve others, only then are we compelled to let go of sorrow. Only then can we imagine how your own light can shine, how much Joy awaits on our playground. Only then do we allow old emotions to recede and we naturally open a door to exit the old and unhealthy emotions, making room for true happiness to take its place."

She suddenly paused, her wings outright, and she glided on the currents for a few moments, struck by an epiphany.

"Jet, sometimes it's easier to hold on to old emotions and beliefs, even when we know they don't serve us well."

She started to cry, coming face to face with her own wounds and her own heavy, internal friction.

He watched as she worked through this cathartic internal process and embraced the changes he was speaking of, impressed at her courage and her vulnerability. He added, "But just coping is a long way from living a full life, much less the life that God wants us to live. We must let go, move on, and find our balance. **If we don't hunt for our own triangle, then nothing changes and we will always get what we have always got! Nothing changes!** As I shared with you in Deep Creek, we must make room for change by letting go of the parts of our past that no longer serve us. We must feed the Good Wolf!"

They flew on. They had no more than an hour left before Tampa Bay would be in sight. Old Radar wanted to punctuate this important point to help Jet make sense of it all. "Jet, may I share another short story that illuminates our choices in life and the impact our choices can have?"

Jet continued looking directly forward as Old Radar spoke. Her silence he interpreted as permission to carry on.

A big, tough samurai warrior once went to see a little monk. "Monk!" he barked, in a voice accustomed to instant obedience. "Teach me about heaven and hell!"

The monk looked up at the mighty warrior and replied with utter disdain, "Teach you about heaven and hell? I couldn't teach you about anything. You're dumb. You're dirty. You're a disgrace, an embarrassment to the samurai class. Get out of my sight. I can't stand you."

The samurai grew furious. He shook with rage, red in the face, speechless with anger. He drew his sword and prepared to slay the monk.

Looking straight into the samurai's eyes, the monk said softly, "That's hell."

The samurai warrior froze, realizing the compassion of the monk who had risked his life to show him hell! The warrior put away his sword and fell to his knees, filled with deep gratitude.

And the monk said softly, "And that is heaven."[2]

2.   Fred Kofman, Ph.D., *Conscious Business: How to Build Value Through Values* (Sounds True, 2013).

Old Radar could see Jet slowly nodding as the story concluded. He then added, "Anger, sorrow, and regret are the most invasive negative emotions the universe brings us. We must all wrestle with these at some point in our lives. But how we process it and work through the intensity defines us.

"In the story I just shared, the samurai warrior carries and uses anger as a tool—it fuels him and allows him to create fear in others. But he knows it's unsustainable and he seeks more from the monk."

He continued, "All anger has a close friend—fear. Fear! When we hold on to anger, we hold on to a deeper internal fear, a source of energy that fuels all anger. The samurai used anger and rage to intimidate others. On the surface we think this is to conquer others and to dominate. But deep down, the anger and rage of the warrior is his own fear of loss, a fear of Love and Joy that he is unwilling to expose himself to. He thinks he is better off alone and doesn't need anyone. He thinks, *Why can't others see this?* He is unwilling to change, as the anger serves him well enough to cope and survive.

"He seeks the monk because he is thirsty for wisdom. Deep down, he is tired of his anger and rage."

As his story closed out, Tampa Bay waters came to view. Jet drafted on the wind currents again.

Jet turned to Old Radar and said, "Radar, you've helped me so much over the last few days. It's me who should be thanking *you* for being my partner and accompanying me to Tampa. I could not have made it without you."

"You are stronger and more able than you can possibly understand, Jet. Trust in your talents and gifts and your journey will always be 'on course.'"

"Pun intended, I'm sure," she said, smiling at him.

CHAPTER 10

So, honk for vision,
teamwork, and trust,

Make space for
change, this is a must.

Be humble in leadership,
it's the source of all care,

You're never alone,
God's flock is midair.

Splashdown

Riddled with lakes, streams, ponds, and separated by a quad of four distinct bays, the Tampa Bay watershed covered almost 6,400 square miles. So impressed by the vastness of the water and the overall look of the area, Jet honked and dropped down to less than 1,000 feet, flying low over the trees during the evening sunset to take it all in.

"How are we ever going to find them?" she shouted over the sounds of the city and human streets below.

Shouting back, "Trust your instincts, Jet—they're *your* flock!"

She banked left, heading to a collection of small lakes and ponds, west of the city central, not more than a mile from the Old Tampa Bay area itself. *Hyde Park* was the name of the area she suddenly remembered from her parents' stories. With no information other than this faint memory, she locked in on Old Radar's advice to use her instinct as her compass. She pointed her beak southwest and kept heading fast in that direction. Old Radar could barely keep up! A feeling of Hope and excitement engulfed her.

Within moments she found her flock of geese, all 30 or so resting on a small central body of water in Hyde Park. They were hunkered down in a beautifully protected area adjacent to Anderson Park, also a neighborhood spot for local humans. A little amazed at her instincts to locate her "family" so quickly, she honked again, and again, and again—with each honk she felt the richness of Joy rise within her, filling her to a point where she was about to "pop."

This cluster of geese she separated from almost four days ago, the group she had spent almost a year closed off from following her parents' disappearance, was now directly below her, honking back and looking up at her with Love. She tucked her wings to descend fast, splashing down in the middle of the gaggle. The geese honked, and danced, and wiggled their tail feathers as she landed among them.

Everyone had a thousand questions: "How are you? Are you hungry? Where did you stop? Are you tired?" As they welcomed her back into the circle, tossing out question after question, she did her best to answer what she could. It was a homecoming she had never imagined, and she recognized how consumed she felt by the feelings of Love and Joy. She had spent so long trying to be alone, privately working through her suffering and loss, and here was her support structure all along. A feeling of Hope inside her suddenly became powerful. She closed her eyes in the middle of all the chaos to appreciate how different it all felt—how different she felt.

In time, an elder of the Leadership Council made her way to the front of the group. The gaggle grew silent. Then, with a calm voice, she presented to Jet the most impactful question, "Hummer?"

"He didn't make it," she said, looking down to reflect on the journey's events and holding back her emotions. She went to speak again but was cut off.

"No," said the elder. "Hummer wants to see you. Can you come with me, Jet?" This was presented in a tone that provided her little choice.

"Wait, Hummer is here?" Her eyes widened. "Hummer is alive!? That can't be..." she stammered. Looking down as if remembering every little detail, she carried on, "But I saw him fall from the sky as the humans aimed their explosives at him. His feathers burst in the air, and he fell."

"Jet, I'm right here."

She looked up from her impassioned monologue with confusion, only to see Hummer moving toward her with a large, warm smile.

"How can this be? The burst feathers. Your fall. You hit the ground—nowhere to be found!"

"I know! And I know you came down to find me. But I couldn't call out, I had to remain silent. Those dogs they sent for me were very close. I got lucky, Jet. The humans only clipped my wing," lifting up his right wing to show the damage. "They made a real mess! And one of the pellets they fired on me hit me in the beak, knocking me out cold." He lifted his head to show a large chip where the impact made a mark on his Canada goose white chin strap.

"But the fall, how did you survive the fall?" Jet asked.

"The storm we navigated earlier must have left some very heavy damage in that area of Pennsylvania. When I came to, almost immediately after landing, I was covered in mud and buried deep within a soft marshland. Fallen tree branches above me helped soften the blow and must have slowed me down. I don't have any other explanation," he paused.

"I just can't believe you are alive...and you actually look better!"

"I was unwell, Jet. And after I cleaned myself up, I was able to jump in a V-formation with another flock who almost carried me here to Tampa. I'm not 100 percent, but I'll make it."

She moved closer, taking it all in, just staring at him. Time just stood still for Jet. She reached out with Love in her heart and hugged Hummer, resting her head under his. "I just can't believe it. I really thought you were gone." Tears began to roll down her face. Still embracing Hummer, she whispered, "Thank you for not leaving me, too."

Hummer relished the hug and her honest, vulnerable emotion. *She's come a long way, in a few days,* he thought.

Jet turned to the group, including the elder, wiped away her tears, and asked, "Where's Radar?"

"Where's who?" replied the elder.

"Radar! Our flying partner who was with me and Hummer!"

They just stared at her. An awkward silence hung in the air. Jet panicked.

"You know, Old Radar? My other *incredible* traveling companion!" almost pleading with them to understand.

Finally, the elder spoke again, "Jet, we don't have a *Radar* in our flock. You completed the migration to Tampa Bay solo. You splashed down here with us solo."

"What? No! Stop it! Radar—Old Radar was on my three-geese flying squad from the very beginning. We were a team of three when we set out from Quebec!"

Hummer, still close, chimed in to help. "No," he said softly and slowly. "Jet, we were broken into teams of twos and threes: an odd grouping this year due to how many of us were migrating. I broke us up into groups based on talent and family pairings. It was just you and me, Jet. I'm sorry. I've never met this...Radar."

"I know you say I landed here just moments ago solo, but that's only because Radar doesn't have the same..." Her voice trailed off, thinking of her next statement. "...The same Love, Hope, and Joy that I do when it comes to having my flock back in my life."

She looked around with a sense of control, unable to find Radar in the crowd of geese. Her own words resonated with her in a way that invited calm.

As if talking to herself, "But I journaled his teaching the entire way. Radar was with me and helped guide me with his leadership, his experience, his stories, and an incredible level of wisdom. Here look!" she grabbed her journal, flipping pages frantically as she passed the triangle, then the poem. After a few moments, with the entire gaggle curious, she lowered her journal and looked up. In those moments she came face to face with the fact that there was not one mention of Old Radar in her notes. She never mentioned him in her journal, but she captured the lessons of Love, Hope, and Joy, along with the wisdom needed to change and find her playground.

"But I don't understand. He was magnificent to me. He was like a..." She looked up, speaking more softly. "He was with me...he guided me...he showed me things about the world and about myself. I don't think I would be here right now if it wasn't for Old Radar."

"I'm sorry, Jet. Whatever or whoever guided you to us here in Tampa is not a member of this flock. We are grateful that you are back, and it's clear to everyone you seem changed, but we just don't know of any 'Radar.'"

She caught her breath to process it all. As she asked herself who he might have been, a heavenly whirl moved through her body. Looking high into the sky, suddenly she saw a large, solo gander flying off into the warm glow of the Florida sunset. He let out a final, soft honk, then he simply vanished into the orange.

Later that night, after all the commotion, the varied discussion, the food, and the festival-like atmosphere, Jet found some quiet time, grabbed her journal, and went off to capture the pivotal moments from her final day—intent on closing out all she had learned from her journey.

She opened to a blank page and wrote:

Your future is bigger

than your past!

Her mind was too busy to keep journaling. Finally, with some time alone to think, she wondered about Old Radar. *He did show up late, but was I the only one aware of his presence? And Hummer never interacted with him? How can this be? He was always with me and always there to help me when*

I needed it. He was beyond wise, and continually able to read my mind. "Radar, who are you?" she said aloud to no one.

Then, suddenly, something strange began to happen on the pages of the journal—the edges of the book began to glow. She rifled through the pages to her sketch of the triangle in the sand. It too was ablaze in an orange glow—like the candles in her dream with her parents as Old Radar served them, and almost the same colorfully warm glow from earlier today when she watched the old gander vanish into the sunset. Her triangle blazed and lit up on the page. Another swirl of energy moved through her. Then, just as suddenly, the glow faded away and the pages returned to the original sketch.

Jet looked up to the sky, took a deep breath, knowing within she was at home with her flock here in Tampa. She now knew what she was meant to do with her talent, energy, passion, and gifts handed down to her through her parents. Feeling stirred but somehow unfazed from this magical moment, she channeled another poem onto the pages of her journal. This time, she started with the title.

Honk

You're blessed in threes,
this we know,

Your serving spirit shows us so.

Not for the glory of the gain,

Not for the hope of fleeting fame,

Not for the shekels it might bring,

You lead because you must sing!

Your gifts will serve you,

and God knows best.

Just trust your radar

and leave the rest.

We thank Him for your

leader's soul,

That song in your heart

you can't control.

Nor should you change

the Joy it brings,

Leave thrones and palaces

to fears and kings!

For what are thrones
and crowns to the ant—
Your gifts bring a Hope
that power can't.
A fading love you do not hold,
It shines more brightly than
candles of gold.
This Love for other, man, beast,
and bee,
Is meant for more,
one day you'll see!

So, honk for vision, teamwork,
and trust,
Make space for change,
this is a must.
Be humble in leadership,
it's the source of all care,

You're never alone,

God's flock is midair.

You're blessed in threes,

this we know,

Love, Hope, and Joy,

onward you go.[3]

Closing her journal, feeling content and deeply aware that her journey to Tampa had been transformative, she took a deep breath, resting, but ready for a future that was to be much bigger than her past.

---

3. The poem "Honk" is from a deconstructed, reconfigured, and repurposed poem, "The Call," written by my great-grandfather, James Edwin Kerr, over 100 years ago.

EPILOGUE

"In the absence of God,
all work is in vain."

—Leo Tolstoy,
Russian writer and philosopher

Closure

In time, Jet was invited to lead the Annual Migration and become part of the Leadership Council. Hummer recommended she step into his role as he stepped down for health reasons. She was unanimously voted in. During her first 90 days, Jet went on a *listening-tour*, attending to and hearing from goose and gander of all ages before framing out her ideas. She was passionate about improving the overall operations of the flock, simultaneously lifting their health and well-being, and helping to adjust flock-strategy.

During the first go-live days on the Council, after completing the listening-tour, Jet honored the elder demographic with a modern approach, giving "voice" to the richness of their wisdom and experience. She felt this had been lost over the years. She proposed a **Wisdom Circle: a selected group of elders meeting regularly to discuss a wide set of dynamics within the flock.** Their agenda was filled with items such as leadership development, succession, family health, culture, and food supply, to name a few.

Jet never truly figured out who Old Radar was, or where he disappeared to after splashing down in Tampa. Some said he was an angel, sent by her parents to remind her of them. Some said he was a guardian angel who entered her life to help her through to Tampa and share wisdom. Others said he was an old friend of her parents helping her along her first migration. Whatever and whoever he was, Jet continued to feel a spiritual connection to the mysticism of Old Radar and honored him by labeling the Wisdom Circles "Radar-Talks." Each monthly meeting considered all current matters with a lens of seven generations. Jet invited the group to serve the **Seventh Generation Principle**, an ancient Iroquois and Native American philosophy she became enamored with after hearing the Two Wolves tale from Old Radar. The approach considered the sustainability of topics and decisions to positively impact seven generations into the future. The closing question at every Radar-Talk was always the same: "As everything here is connected, have we missed anything or anyone?"

To honor her parents, Jet successfully ran a project to explore the same territory along the coast of Maine that once claimed them from her. **Through a project she named *Dreaming*,** a select team set out and found suitable terrain along the Maine coastline to safely house the entire flock for a few extra weeks each year before departing south to Tampa. Never again did they face an early winter or a seasonal hurricane to threaten the gaggle. The impact on morale throughout the flock was surprisingly overwhelming: **the geese felt heard, and they felt safe**.

The lessons from Mother Nature with her examples of teamwork, collaboration, and role clarity were supplied to

Jet with examples of best-practice from other species, and these lessons were never lost on her. Jet was impacted so deeply she shared her experiences with the community in a series of talks and articles written from the heart. From this, the flock was sparked with innovation and voted to **form a *biomimicry program*—investing time and resources to study nature to uncover more lessons they might apply within.** The aim of the program was to emulate models and systems found in nature that could help solve complex problems.

Finally, when the time was right, she established a *leadership development program*, supported by a *mentoring program*. Each program was based on the principle and doctrine of the triangle to help younger generations find their own internal balance as they explored Love, Hope, and Joy. Combined, these programs acted as a filter for a succession of talent to the Leadership Council, allowing smooth transitions when the time came for a member to step down.

Most of all, Jet *flattened the traditional hierarchy*, erasing traditional measures of status and rank with merit-based programs, building in collaboration and innovation systems to allow all members of the flock to feel more engaged, empowered, and encouraged to learn and grow. Leveraging the core concept of "visibility" and "team communication" present in the team V-formation used by geese when traveling, she **modernized the operating structure to tap into information and data available throughout the entire**

flock: no longer the sole domain of the Leadership Council.

Over time, the flock developed their own mantra, **"You grow. We grow." They built language and meaning to the idea that we progress (as a whole) as each of us progresses at the personal level.** They understood the importance of this symmetrical growth.

In short order, the flock flourished and performed better together, multiplying in numbers—the measure of the flock swelled to twice the size in under three years. Word was out across the territories and states land that this gaggle from Sainte-Petronille, Quebec, was the most vibrant and impactful flock in the land. It was never her intention, but Jet became known to others as a true leader who rebuilt the traditional structures and systems with vision and purpose to serve others.

Jet lived the rest of her days by sharing **servant leadership principles** that came from her own journey **with Love, Hope, and Joy.** She could never understand how or why she was widely recognized for simply helping others grow. She often said as she grew older, "I really didn't do much. I just provided a framework for others to grow and become their own authentic self through roles and structures that mattered."

Today, flocks from all over the world visit Sainte-Petronille, Quebec, to study Jet's unusual, yet modern leadership model.

ACKNOWLEDGMENTS

With Gratitude

The first person I want to acknowledge here is Dr. Tom Saunders, who has been incredibly important to me throughout the writing process. Your experience as a writer, editor, a pastor, and a trainer in leadership has helped me stay accountable from the start. But most of all, I am grateful for your deep passion for the Lord. Tom, you make a difference!

I'm overly grateful and indebted to a few dear friends who have had access to advanced drafts of *Honk*. To you, Marc Kolp, Sheila Caldis, and Dean DiSibio, Colonel U.S. Army (Ret.), I am in your debt for the ideas, feedback, and edits in helping me bring this story to life. Your patience with me during this work was notable.

I want to thank my parents, who many years ago encouraged me to do something bigger with my writings and "silly poems." Art and Mary, my fun-loving and happy parents, may you rest in peace—knowing that I (forever) heard you.

At the risk of cliché, I thank my colleagues and friends from StratWealth, an award-winning, independent wealth management firm. You allowed me to lead as Chief Executive for almost five years before selling, before integrating with Wealthspire Advisors. You trusted in me to use all my gifts and talents, and together we transformed the business, improved lives, spread Love, Hope, and Joy, and handled a ton of change together—highs, lows, and new beginnings. Servant leadership became my playground—operating with so many different generations under one roof, we built a truly beautiful business in a remarkable amount of time.

Naturally, and most of all, I give special thanks to my wife and our four kids. Anne, your support and encouragement to "get it done" is worthy of a book on its own. You are the only one on earth who knows this small story has been in my head for over a decade. Your comment one day as I vacillated about the work will stick with me forever: "God only yells so loud." You are my "Radar" and I love you for that (and so much more). To my four children—Jaylen, Charlotte, Jackson, and Oscar—I could not be prouder of you. It's a joy to watch you grow into the adults that await you around each corner. I can only pray that I bring you the Joy that you bring me (you are my legacy of Love, Hope, and Joy).

My friend Joe Brooks, thank you for your creative graphics and design of the cover. You nailed it, my friend!

The final poem in the book, "Honk," is translated and reconstructed from a poem, "The Call," written by my great-grandfather, James Edwin Kerr (I'm named after him). Mr. Kerr lived over 100 years ago and remains notable today in South Carolina for his written works. Thank you, sir; your life of poetry has played a role in my path!

The Call

I am a poet, this I know.
Because my spirit tells me so.
Not for the glory of the game
Not for the hope of fleeting fame
Not for the shekels it might bring
I sing because I have to sing!

God called me and my God knows best,
I trust Him and I leave the rest.
I thank Him for my dreamer's soul,
The song in my heart cannot control.
Nor would I change the joy it brings
For thrones and palaces of kings!

For what are thrones and crowns to me—
Who owns the world and all I see?
No facing tinsel that they hold
Can match my starts—my lilies gold!
And so I bless my Master's way
And listen to my soul and say:

"For this is great wealth Thou gavest me,
This love for man and beast and bee—
The boon to feel in sky and sod
They hand touch mine—I thank Thee God."

—James E. Kerr

BONUS MATERIAL

Fear holds us all back from what we are truly capable of. It's easy to shrink or stay inside our comfort zone, yet fear is mostly a man-made and a self-imposed construct.

Interview with the Author

The following is an excerpt of an interview with the author, Jim DeCarlo.

> **Interviewer: Clever story, Jim. How did you come up with the idea of this book?**

Jim: They say, "You don't find a book, a book finds you." With *Honk*, I can say the same thing—this story found me!

The concepts in this story have been working their way through me for almost 15 years. At many points, early in my career, my involvement in leadership training courses often compared our human social structures and organizational design with the wider aspects of nature, insects, and animals—specifically noting how nature effortlessly organizes itself into teams and sub-teams to operate. My burning question has always been *"Why do humans complicate it?"* This idea of geese flying south sharing how they overcome personal and group challenges came to me many years ago...and it stuck.

Interviewer: Why did it take you 15 years? What held you up?

Jim: Change can be hard. And writing about change, even on a personal level, is harder.

I know that I've wrestled with change over the years. Certain amounts of family and workplace "shock" have had their impact on me. I had to learn, personally, to let go to make space (inside) for such life transitions I faced. I always felt it was God's plan for me to learn from these events, not be held back by them.

I think at the most basic level it was fear that held up this story being shared. Fear holds us all back from what we are truly capable of. It's easy to shrink or stay inside our comfort zone, yet fear is mostly a man-made and a self-imposed construct. Even cognizant of my irrationality with fear, it's crazy that it took this long to produce *Honk*.

Interviewer: What fear are you talking about, and how did you overcome it?

Jim: I tried to trick myself that my reason for not banging on the keyboard was a lack of time (my wife, my family, my work, another project). It moved to a fear of starting the *Honk* journey and not finishing it. A life of limbo. But, if I'm honest with myself, it was a fear that my work stunk, that I can't write, and

the story is "mumbo-jumbo" that nobody will find construc-
tive. I was anchored in a fear of failure.

This will sound cliché, but I found my voice and my own
"balance" with Love, Hope, and Joy, and suddenly I had to
write! It was no longer a book for others, but a story of a
modern leadership journey I wanted to share. I hope it res-
onates with leaders all over the world, but if *Honk* impacts
just one person or one team in a positive way, then it's been
worth the work.

I've lost all fear of rejection as a writer while, in parallel,
the very process of writing brought me into my playground.
Can't ask for much more!

> **Interviewer:** Love, Hope, and Joy are presented to the
> reader through the shape of a triangle. Can you talk
> more about this?

Jim: Sure. The geometric shape of the triangle is found
everywhere. We can see it all around us throughout the arc
of time and history—such as religion, architecture, in business strategy and in war.

In life, we are all equally on a journey to live a balanced
life. Balance is in demand all around us. We balance work,
family, and learning. We balance exercise, recovery, and
nutrition. We balance protein, fats, and carbohydrates. We

study in balance with math, science, and history. It goes on and on! Yet nothing really speaks to the breakdown of finding balance as it relates to our God-given gifts and talents. Everyone, of all ages, is left to figure it out on their own.

Introduce this complex system to teams and business and it's no wonder so many groups are dysfunctional, while the research around us says employees are less engaged than ever. The leader is unhappy, following an outdated leadership program where they use tools to control people around them, and the people are unhappy because they don't feel valued. It doesn't have to be this way!

Over time, great businesses, remarkable humans, infamous cultures, and long-standing social structures teach us a form of balance. But you must look to see it! To me it is broken down into Love, Hope, and Joy.

- The framing of **Love** as the most fundamental ingredient, at the base of the triangle, has always been the most important to me. Love, above all, is a verb, not a noun. It's the action we take with and for others that feeds and nourishes us.

- **Joy** is second. Joy is family, friends and community where being in healthy relationship is required to expose our core happiness.

- These two, when equal in strength, feed and give life to **Hope**. Hope is where we find our *playground*. When in our playground we feel at home and free to become a beacon of light for others, regardless of our role, job, station, age, or status. We matter, and we know it. We leave our legacy without trying.

My executive coach, Sebastion Little, was the first to shine a light and call it "my playground." (I'm blessed to have him in my life.)

Interviewer: And you think this is a more modern leadership model, how?

Jim: Yup! Leadership today often fails to empower and stretch people to grow. Too often business treats people as if they are expendable units, not supporting their true gifts and talents in the team. They are not built for change. This drags on the person and in turn drags on the business.

As a father of four, a mentor in my local county's leadership program, and a CEO within the finance industry, I see today's leadership often struggling to know what's important, using a traditional command and control model to make people perform, and wondering why teams don't perform like they should. But change is constant today and I am a firm believer that we need a better way of getting everyone to embrace it.

Old school is just that—old and outdated. To win today you need to be nimble and everyone needs a hand on the wheel in some shape and form.

Interviewer: You often mention that we all must deal with change. Can you share more?

Jim: Jet's early challenge of needing to let go of anger for the loss of her parents is really a metaphor for any obstacle or personal event from our past, magnified and held onto, that defines how we operate today. Loss, poor upbringing, low social status, money or the lack thereof, failed business, failed marriage, and personal injury can all be life-affecting. Each of us faces obstacles in some form or another. How we deal with these defines us. If we don't find a way to process events or people that hurt us or try to hold us back, then it keeps us from reaching our full potential.

Honk, through Jet, shows us how we might deal with these issues and develop a framework for personal change.

Interviewer: They say an author writes themselves into the story in some way. Who is Jim DeCarlo in this story?

Jim: Tricky question, but I think you see a little of me in all three characters of *Honk*. As a journey-man on this earthly walk, I'm just like Jet, dealing with issues and challenges and learning from others along the way. Then, at times, I'm also Radar: sharing my experiences and life lessons with younger generations. But I'm also Hummer—a chosen leader and pushing people to lift their game and live into the person they are meant to me. I can only hope I'm balanced enough to state my mistakes and equally willing and able to step aside when others are ready to lead.

Interviewer: If the reader can take one thing from the book, what would that be?

Jim: That's hard to answer. I think the book lands on different people in different ways depending on where they are in the arc of life and leadership. I believe the key to all success is the approach we take to other people: few understand how important this is. Building a beautiful business requires the leader to have a balance of Love, Hope, and Joy—getting people to come work with more than just their hands and their feet, but their hearts and their minds. That's magic!

But if I had to pick one key message it's that *everything is connected*—people, nature, the planet, God, and the idea of Love, Hope, and Joy. We live large when we understand these concepts and work to live and lead harmoniously within our playground.

> **Interviewer: This is your first book; will there be more to come?**

Jim: This story just came to me and fell out onto the pages. I don't know if I could ever write a book without that type of "flow"—so if that flow shows up again, I'm ready to bang it out. I have a few ideas, but they are very different to *Honk*.

For now, I just want to share the key messages and help others find their "balance"—that's my playground.

Everything is connected—people, nature, the planet, God, and the idea of Love, Hope, and Joy. We live large when we understand these concepts and work to live and lead harmoniously within our playground.

Everything is
connected - people,
nature, the planet,
God, and the idea
of Love, Hope and
Joy. We live large
when we understand
these concepts and
work to live and act
harmoniously within
our playground.

About
the Author

J im DeCarlo is a recognized leader with over three decades in the financial services industry, globally.

Jim is a recognized CEO who has worked with some of the finest, privately owned, wealth management teams in the US, and some of the largest investment management platforms throughout Australia. As an entrepreneur, Jim coached dozens of small business owners, firsthand, on matters of process improvement, change management, and leadership.

Today Jim is an international dual citizen of Australia and the USA – sharing time between his two homes as he works his "playground."

Tomorrow's leadership matters today. How to lead in a world of change and uncertainty is where true leadership shines. We hope the story of Honk, and the insights shared, provide a framework for transforming your own style and helps drive organizational change.

Stay in touch:

 Honk-leadership.com

 linkedin.com/in/ jimdecarlo

 @jdc2122

 @jdecarlo9030

 jdc2122@gmail.com

Honk on!

THANK YOU FOR READING THIS BOOK!

If you found any of the information helpful, please take a few minutes and leave a review on the bookselling platform of your choice.

BONUS GIFT!

Don't forget to sign up to try our newsletter and grab your free personal development ebook here:

soundwisdom.com/classics